When Pigs Fly

Story by Valerie Coulman

Pictures by Rogé

Lobster Press™

Coulman, Valerie, 1969-
When Pigs Fly
Text © 2001 Valerie Coulman
Illustrations © 2001 Rogé Girard

Published by
Lobster Press™
1620 Sherbrooke Street West, Suites C & D
Montréal, Québec   H3H 1C9
Tel. (514) 904-1100 • Fax (514) 904-1101
www.lobsterpress.com

Publisher: Alison Fripp
Editor: Jane Pavanel
Book Designer: Shari Blaukopf
Production Manager: Tammy Desnoyers

Distributed in the United States by:
Publishers Group West
1700 Fourth Street
Berkeley, CA 94710

Distributed in Canada by:
Raincoast Books
9050 Shaughnessey Street
Vancouver, BC V6P 6E5

We acknowledge the financial support of the Government of Canada through the Book Publishing Industry Development Program (BPIDP) for our publishing activities.

The Canada Council | Le Conseil des Arts
for the Arts | du Canada

We acknowledge the support of the Canada Council for the Arts for our publishing program.

National Library of Canada Cataloguing in Publication Data
Coulman, Valerie, 1969-
    When pigs fly

ISBN 1-894222-36-9

    I. Girard, Rogé, 1972- II. Title.

PS8555.O82295W48 2001   jC813'.6   C2001-900242-2
PZ7.C8303Wh 2001

The illustrations were rendered in acrylics
The text was typeset in Veljovic
Printed and bound in Canada.

To my brother Pierre, who taught me that to draw is to fly. R.G.

In a meadow near the city lived
a cow named Ralph.

Ralph wanted his dad to buy him a bicycle.

"But Ralph," his dad said, "cows don't ride bikes."
"Not yet they don't," Ralph replied.

Ralph asked and asked and asked his dad
for a bike, but his dad said

no

and no

and no!

Finally he said, "Okay, Ralph, I'll buy you a bike . . . when pigs fly."

Ralph thought about that. Then one day, while playing with some friends, he had an idea. But first he had to learn how to fly a helicopter.

"Why do you want to fly a helicopter, Ralph?"
asked his friend Morris. "Cows don't fly."
"Not yet they don't," said Ralph.
Morris looked puzzled.
Ralph explained, "My dad said he'd buy me
a bike when pigs fly."
"But Ralph," Morris said, "pigs don't fly."
"Not yet they don't," said Ralph.

Morris looked even more puzzled.
Ralph laughed. "If I learn to fly
a helicopter," he said, "I can take some
pigs for a ride. Then I can have a bike."
"Ralph," Morris said, "cows
don't ride bikes."
"Not yet they don't," said Ralph.

The next day Ralph went to the airport. He saw a
woman loading suitcases onto an airplane.
"Excuse me," said Ralph. "Is there someone here who
can teach me how to fly a helicopter?"

Millie looked a little surprised.
"Umm . . . Bill can," she said, "but . . . cows
don't fly helicopters."
"Not yet they don't," Ralph smiled.

Ralph went to see Bill.
"Why do you want to learn to fly
a helicopter?" Bill asked.
"When I learn to fly a helicopter, I can take
some pigs for a ride," Ralph explained. "My dad
said that when pigs fly, I can have a bike."
"Ralph," said Bill, "do you know that cows
don't ride bicycles?"
"Not yet they don't," said Ralph.

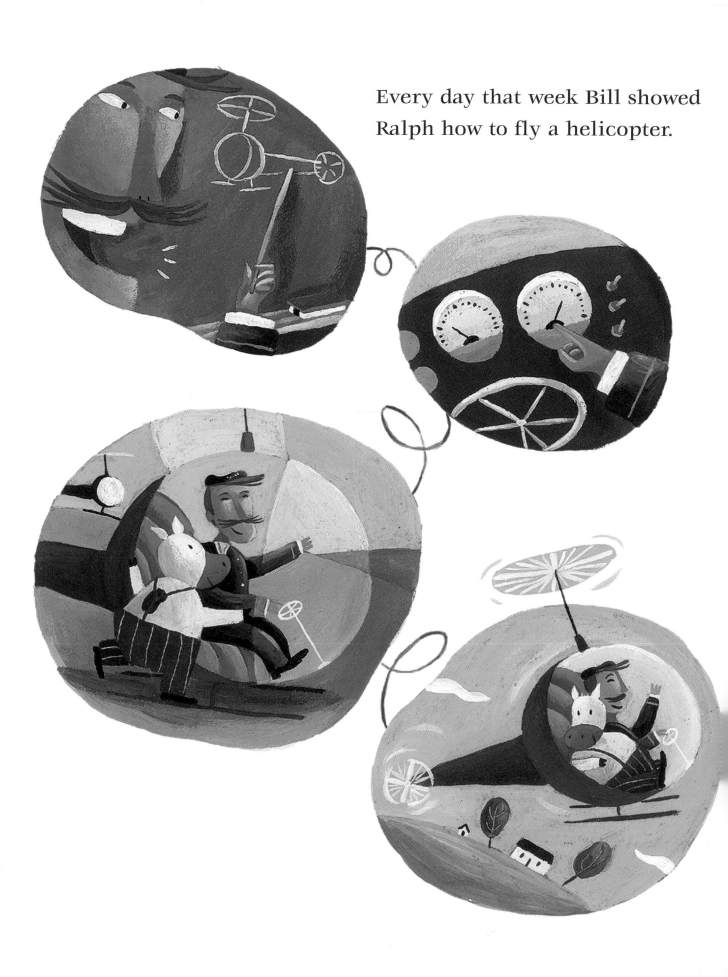

Every day that week Bill showed Ralph how to fly a helicopter.

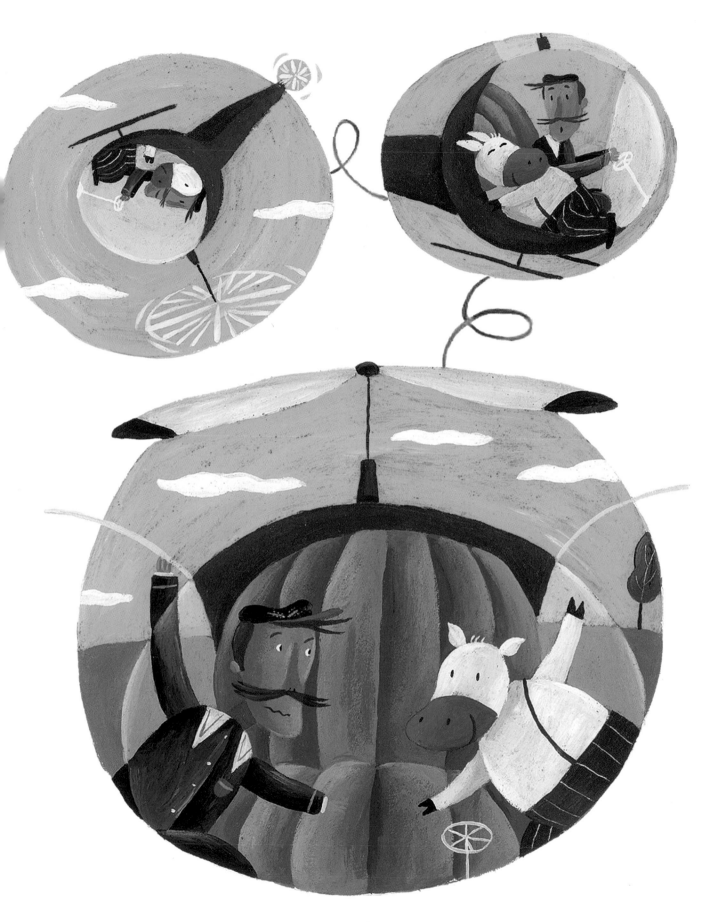

Ralph learned to fly up and down
and backwards and forwards.
He even learned to fly in circles.

It was a very exciting week
for Ralph. Sometimes
it was exciting for Bill, too.

As soon as his lessons were finished, Ralph went to see
his friends Julia and Margaret.
"Can I take you for a helicopter ride?" he asked.
Julia's eyes opened wide. Margaret's mouth opened wide.
"But Ralph," they said, "we're pigs. Pigs don't fly."
"Not yet they don't," answered Ralph.

The very next morning Ralph took Julia and
Margaret for a ride in a helicopter. The circles made
Julia a little dizzy and Margaret liked going up better
than down, but they both had fun.

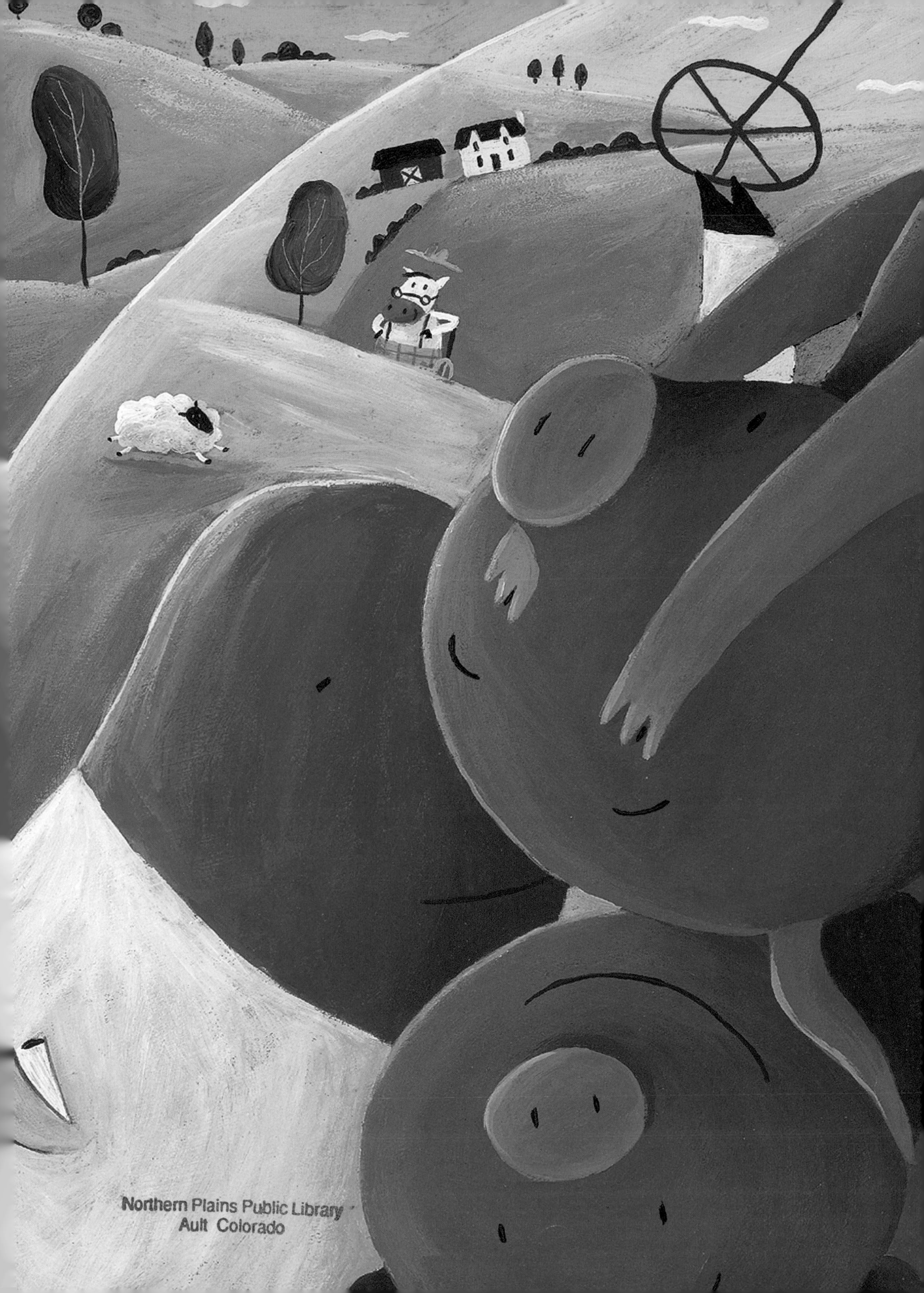

When the helicopter landed Ralph said
thank you to Julia and Margaret.
"I have to get home," he said. "My dad is
going to buy me a bike."

"A bike?" said Margaret.
But Ralph was already gone.
"Ralph," Julia called after him, "cows
don't ride bikes." His answer came
back to them,

"Not yet they don't."